ORLAND PARK PUBLIC LIBRARY

3 1315 00324 1945

P9-EMG-447

DEC   2000

DISCARD

ORLAND PARK PUBLIC LIBRARY
AILEEN S. ANDREW MEMORIAL
14760 PARK LANE
ORLAND PARK, ILLINOIS 60462
349-8138

DEMCO

TESTING MISS MALARKEY

To grandson Joshua Sidney Finchler, may your life be filled with as much joy as you have brought to ours. —J. F.

To Big Pat and the Vizzard Family. —K. O.

Text copyright © 2000 by Judy Finchler
Illustrations copyright © 2000 by Kevin O'Malley

All rights reserved.
No part of this book may be reproduced or transmitted in any form or by any means,
electronic or mechanical, including photocopying, recording, or by any information storage and retrieval system,
without permission in writing from the Publisher.

All the characters and events portrayed in this work are fictitious.

First published in the United States of America in 2000 by
Walker Publishing Company, Inc.

Published simultaneously in Canada by Fitzhenry and Whiteside,
Markham, Ontario L3R 4T8

Library of Congress Cataloging-in-Publication Data

Finchler, Judy.
    Testing Miss Malarkey / Judy Finchler ; illustrations by Kevin O'Malley.
        p. cm.
    Summary: Although the teachers, the principal, and parents say The Test is not important,
their actions tell another story.
    ISBN 0-8027-8737-1 (hardback) — ISBN 0-8027-8739-8 (reinforced)
    [1. Achievement tests—Fiction. 2. Schools—Fiction.] I. O'Malley, Kevin, 1961– ill. II. Title.

PZ7.F495666 Te 2000
[E]—dc21

                                                                00-028100

Book design by Sophie Ye Chin

Printed in Hong Kong

2 4 6 8 10 9 7 5 3 1

TESTING MISS MALARKEY

Judy Finchler
Illustrations by Kevin O'Malley

WALKER & COMPANY ✳ NEW YORK

ORLAND PARK PUBLIC LIBRARY

Miss Malarkey is a good teacher. Usually she's really nice. But a couple of weeks ago she started acting a little weird. She started talking about THE TEST: The Instructional Performance Through Understanding test. I think Miss Malarkey said it was called the "I.P.T.U." test.

But Miss Malarkey said THE TEST wasn't that important. She said it wouldn't affect our report cards. It wouldn't mean extra homework. And if we didn't do well, we'd still go on to the next grade.

At recess we played Multiplication Mambo. Each class got new CD roms called "There's Something About Decimals." After lunch we played Funny Phonics. Miss Malarkey said you never know what's going to be on THE TEST.

The closer we got to "THE TEST DAY," the weirder things got. When I brought the attendance sheets to the office, I heard Principal Wiggins yelling about pencils.

The cafeteria lady, Mrs. Slopdown, took away the potato chips and served only fish.

My food usually goes right to my stomach.

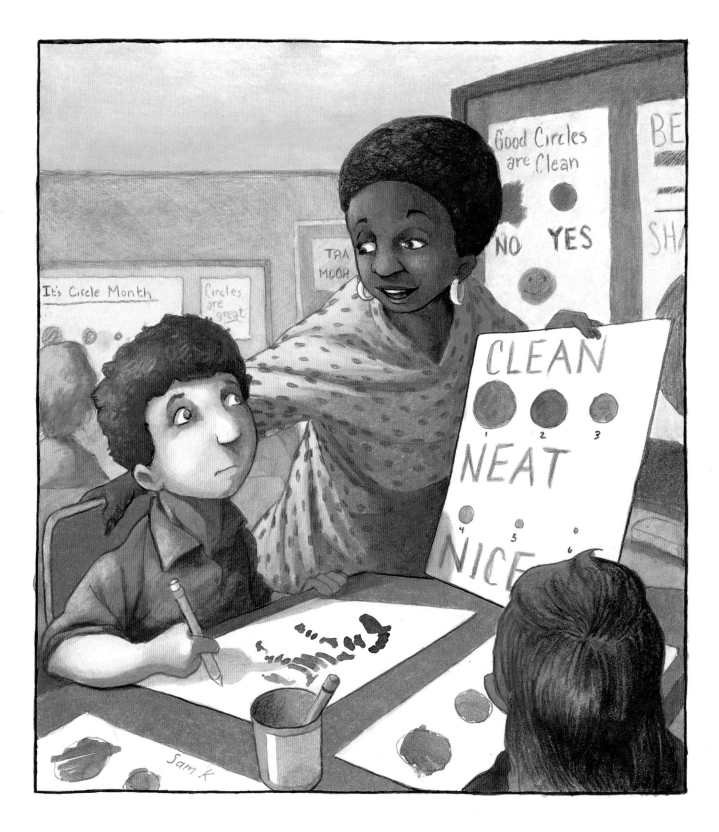

In art we each made posters about THE TEST. Mrs. Magenta also showed us how to color in all those little circles they put on tests.

During gym we didn't play baseball or even exercise. Mr. Fittanuff said we had to prepare our minds and bodies for THE TEST. We all learned something about meditating and about something called "yogurt." Like I said, things were getting pretty weird at school. I got to thinking THE TEST was sort of important.

Even my mom knew about THE TEST. When she read me my bedtime story, I had to complete a ditto and give the main idea before I could go to sleep.

324 1945

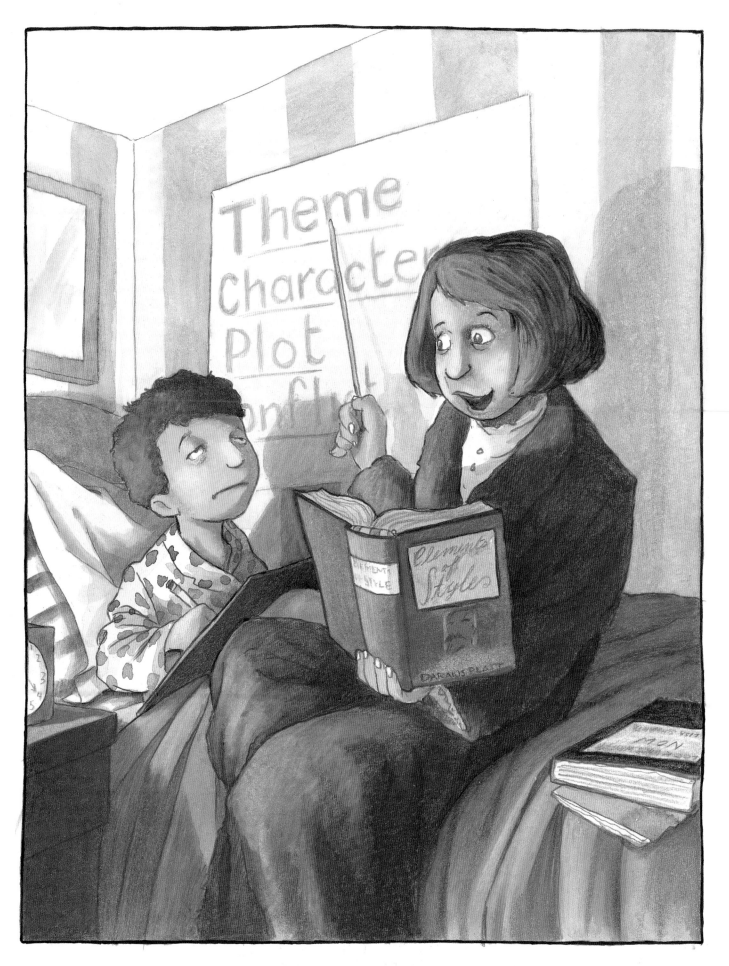

ORLAND PARK PUBLIC LIBRARY

Mom started making me eat a really big breakfast. For lunch she packed me a Power Bar 2000. When I got to school, I traded Adam for a fat-free bran muffin. He traded with Hanna for a Baggie of carrot sticks. Hanna didn't want the Power Bar so she asked her best friend, Meredith, if she would trade for her apple. Somehow someone must have wanted the apple, and I'm not sure what happened but I had the Power Bar 2000 again.

One night Mom took me to a PTA meeting. A man was there talking about THE TEST. He wasn't a teacher or a parent or even the principal, but whoever he was he seemed to think THE TEST was very important. So did the parents.

The day of THE TEST the janitor, Mr. Surley, closed off the whole hallway. You couldn't even walk down it unless you had a pass. And you had to whisper. Miss Malarkey had to whisper the secret password to Mr. Surley before she could go to Room 10.

TESTERS ONLY

NO TALKING!!

IPTU - TESTING - AREA -

BE PREPARED

DANGER

That morning there were more teachers than kids waiting for the nurse.

Miss Malarkey's job was to hand out the No. 2 pencils and the scratch paper. She looked like she didn't get enough sleep. Principal Wiggins was keeping the time. We couldn't even touch THE TEST until he waved the flag. When it was time to start, he waved the flag so hard, something happened to his hair.

THE TEST took forever.
It took two whole
days. My friend Carmine
got in trouble for not
using his scratch paper
the right way. I thought
his ninja warrior looked
pretty good, though.

Miss Malarkey caught Barry with his
baseball cards.

Morgan got a stomachache
and had to go to the nurse.
The hall monitor gave her
such a hard time, she threw
up right in the hall.

When Miss Malarkey said
to erase all your pencil marks,
Janet erased her whole test.

Principal Wiggins was in the room for
a while, but he had a stomachache
and had to go to the nurse. I hope he
didn't throw up in the hall too.

After THE TEST everybody got prizes and had treats and we got extra recess. Even Steven, who fell asleep two times during THE TEST. Miss Malarkey looked wiped out, and she didn't even take THE TEST.

It's been a long time since we took THE TEST. Things are back to normal. Principal Wiggins isn't yelling quite as much. The cafeteria lady started serving potato chips again. Mom's packing me good old peanut butter and jelly sandwiches. And Miss Malarkey is letting her fingernails grow real long. I guess THE TEST really wasn't that important after all.

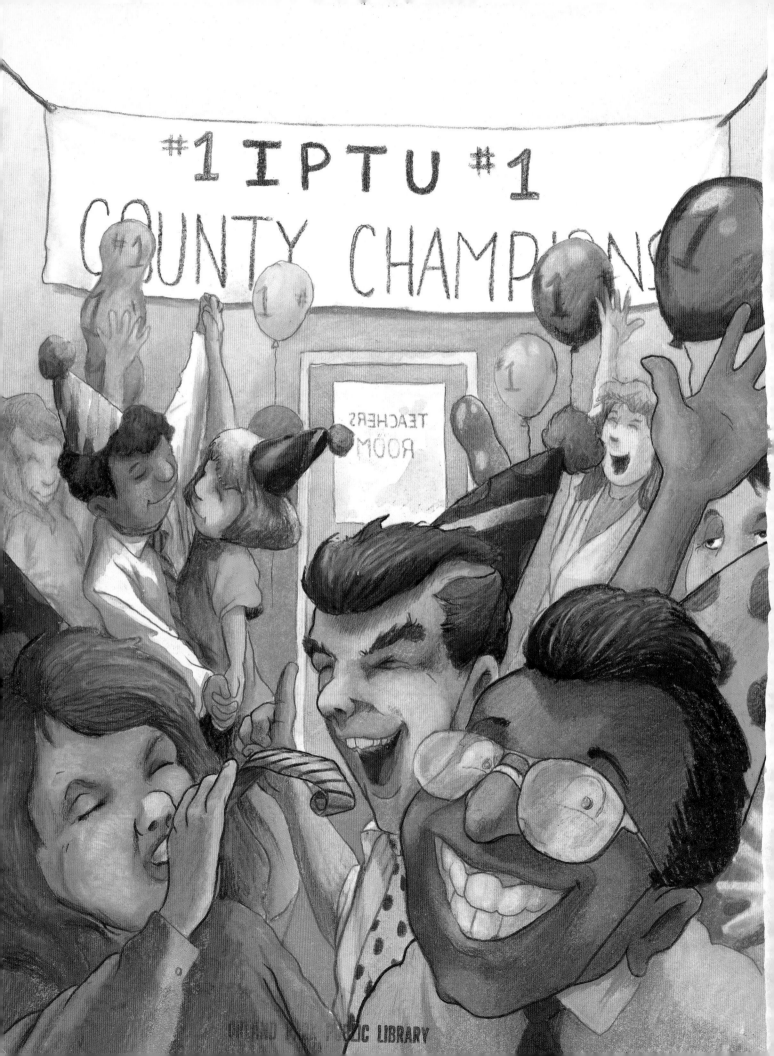
ORLAND PARK PUBLIC LIBRARY

Phillips

KNAPP

Stauffer

ROGERS FORGE

Pacwill

Mirzara

McDonald golden

Schwartz-King

← Flanaway →

Kraft-McVey

EASTON Emily

Palermo